Friends Forever in My Heart

Judith Adele Yarbrough

Friends Forever in My Heart

Copyright © 2013 by Judith Adele Yarbrough

The Place for Words Press
200 Great Road, Suite 254A, Bedford, MA 01730

For all works of fiction represented in this book, all of the characters, names, incidents, organizations and dialogue are either the products of the author's imagination or are used fictitiously.

Edited by Mindy Pollack-Fusi

Book cover design by Robert Fichtel

ISBN: 978-0-9837397-4-6

DEDICATION

❖ *My sister Mil who believed I could do whatever I put my mind to.*

❖ *My writing teacher/mentor, Mindy, who helped me fulfill a dream.*

And special thanks to: my early readers, Charlotte Christen, Mary Flatley, Jill Kutchin; Leslie Wittman for copy editing; and Denise Waldron and Kelly Donivan for their wonderful reviews.

Judith Adele Yarbrough

CONTENTS

Friends are the sunshine of life.
-- *by John Hay*

*A friend is someone who reaches for
your hand but touches your heart.*
-- *by Anonymous*

PROLOGUE

THE GIRLS/FRIENDSHIP FOUND

This is a story about the bonds of friendship. It is a story of how four young women came together in the mid-1970s, drawn together by a common karma and a mutual need to connect with girlfriends for girl talk and girl fun. Two were in their mid-thirties when we met, one in her early twenties, and I was around thirty. We all had men in our lives—husbands, ex-husbands, boyfriends—but this is largely a story about the times we girls spent together.

In a way, this is a love story; well it once was, and for a very long time, but it is also a story about how love shifts and changes throughout the years and, sometimes, even best friends slip apart.

On these pages, you will meet The Girls: Marilyn, Charlotte, Bella, and me, Jodi.

This story dates back nearly forty years, when I went to work for a bank, working the evening shift,

6 to 11 pm. I was in charge of bank statements, Charlotte and Marilyn were check filers, and Bella, the youngest, did all the Xeroxing of customer statements. Some fifteen other women worked at the bank, but we four just seemed to connect, maybe for the simple reason that we all had the same coffee breaks. We would sit and talk about our lives twice a day for fifteen minutes. When we first met, they were all married and had babies; I was the only single one. As time went on, we met outside of work more and more often, going out for dinner or drinks, or meeting at Marilyn's spacious home, celebrating something special or nothing at all. Occasionally the men in our lives were included, but not very often. It was Girl Time! And it was always fun—well, almost always.

Maybe our friendship sparked because of some deeper reason that we may never know. For me, the friendship left footprints on my heart, and these friends from long ago remain in my soul as "Friends Forever."

CHAPTER 1

THE SURPRISE BIRTHDAY PARTY

I am sixty-nine now, but I will never forget the party that The Girls planned for us on my fortieth birthday, because those years were among my favorite. Marilyn, Charlotte and Bella cooked up quite a plan to celebrate my special day. All I was told was to be ready by 7 pm, no questions asked.

I decided to wear black dress pants, and after trying on several different tops, I chose a multi-colored sparkling sweater—a bit more dramatic than my usual conservative way of dressing. I also slid on my black strappy heels, which made me taller than The Girls for the first time. I felt that maybe, along with the sparkling sweater, I would really stand out. I even decided to put on a bit of makeup to really shock them. (Marilyn—the flirt of the group—certainly gave Revlon a lot of business, but the rest of us usually wore little or none.) I added a silver necklace and some bangle bracelets, and as I looked in the mirror, I said to myself, "stunning."

At 6:55 pm, the apartment bell rang. Back then I lived alone in a high-rise apartment, and I always loved my bell; when it rang I felt like I was in London listening to Big Ben. I announced through the intercom that I would be right down. I could hear joyous laughter in the background.

As I exited the elevator into the lobby, they all chimed versions of, "My God, she is sparkling tonight!" I felt on top of the world.

Immediately, Marilyn rushed up with a blindfold. "Jodi, put this on before we take you outside," she said, adding, in a serious tone, "I'm only letting you borrow this for a moment; this is my special sleeping blindfold for my beauty sleep." We all laughed as I slipped it on and they held my hand and led me outside.

After they guided me down three stairs, Marilyn removed the blindfold and they all yelled, "Surprise!" A handsome older white-haired gentleman held open a limousine door. I could not believe my eyes! We were all screaming and laughing like a bunch of teenagers. The driver, Stanley, seemed as excited as we were.

After snapping numerous pictures, Marilyn announced, "We have to include Stanley in our pictures!" So we snapped another bunch.

Finally, we climbed into the limo, still laughing and talking, and the first thing I noticed was a bottle of my favorite wine sitting in a bucket of ice. It had always been a joke with The Girls that I'm the only person they know who needs red wine chilled. A red wine is supposed to be "room temperature," Bella, who was of Italian descent, always said. We asked Stanley to wait a moment before starting to drive so we could make a toast, as none of us wanted to spill any wine on our lovely clothes.

We poured the wine, and Bella said, "Per il Birthday Girl, il nostro più caro amico." (To the birthday girl, our dearest friend.)

I had no idea where we were going, but as we headed in the direction of Boston, I had a feeling it was to the North End. We always had great times there, and at our favorite restaurant, Dolce Vita, they sat us no matter how long the line was outside, since we had dined there so often. That's when you know you certainly are special!

Sure enough, Anthony, the owner of Dolce Vita, was waiting at the door. As the limo pulled up, everyone in the restaurant glanced out the door and windows, probably expecting someone of importance, and surely that night we felt like stars. As we climbed out, Anthony said, "Ciao ragazze" (hello girls). He gave us each a kiss on both cheeks, then led us inside.

A bottle of wine sat in the center of our favorite table, compliments of Anthony. The Girls had already picked the menu: Antipasto, Homemade Minestrone Soup, Chicken Cutlets with Linguine Pasta, and Tiramisu for dessert. Anthony told us we were looking younger and younger every time he saw us, and Marilyn, the shapely, beautiful blond who always flirted whether she was in a relationship or not, just giggled away as usual. Bella loved to go to Dolce Vita, as Anthony always spoke Italian to her. We always felt he was flirting with her, even though he knew she was married (and so was he). Marilyn always wanted Bella to teach her a few words so she could join in. Not going to happen. Charlotte, the more reserved, and less emotional of the bunch, went along with everything, quietly enjoying the moment—and appreciating a night out without her husband and young children.

The food started to arrive, and the aromas filled the air. The antipasto was plentiful, the soup sublime, the cutlets crispy and tender, and the pasta was cooked "al dente," just as we liked it.

After our delicious meal, we were all talking at the same time and didn't notice the waitress walking toward us with a fleet of waiters holding a tiramisu cake with sparklers on top. Everyone started singing "Happy Birthday," including some restaurant patrons, but the ultimate surprise was Anthony's brother coming over with his violin to play "Happy Birthday" to me. We all made a wish on my tiramisu, and I was sure that The Girls and I were wishing the same thing—hoping we would always be together. I loved each of them, always accepting them just the way they were, with all of their unique qualities and idiosyncrasies.

Toward the end of the evening, although we were filled to capacity, we still ordered a cappuccino, the frothing, warm milk on top capping the night with creamy perfection.

"What a wonderful evening," we all said, and we thanked Anthony for his many hospitalities. Marilyn made a call to Stanley to come and get his Girls.

As we were driving out of Boston, we heard an

occasional honking of horns at our car and Charlotte said, "It must be because of the limo, plus they can see the lovely ladies inside."

I was first to be dropped off, and everyone climbed out of the car to hug and kiss me goodbye, and my eye caught something on the back of the limo: a sign saying, "Birthday Girl Inside." That was the reason for the honking of the cars!

It was after midnight as I rode the elevator up to my apartment, so happy about such a wonderful evening! The Girls were an integral, spicy part of my life, and I felt lucky to have them as close friends.

CHAPTER 2

CHARLOTTE AND THE SAD SECRET

Charlotte had grown up the oldest of nine siblings. She always complained that she was like the Mother; she had to take care of everyone and couldn't wait to meet her Prince Charming who would take her away from all that.

Well, sure enough, before we all met, along came Prince Charming (as she thought), and since she couldn't wait to get married, it was a very quick relationship and they had a very small wedding. (The Girls and I assumed she was pregnant already, because that little girl came quite quickly according to the stories she told us!) He was a traveling salesman for a huge pharmaceutical company that soon promoted him to handle the overseas markets. She couldn't have been more excited about the thought of traveling all the time although she didn't, often, at first.

The Girls and I had a few encounters with

Charlotte and Tony, her Prince Charming, at birthdays and holiday get-togethers, and a couple of times he joined us for lunch. Each time, something in the back of our minds nagged at us and we suspected he was a little "shady." Charlotte would never have listened to us, as she was living the fine life. So we zipped it.

Apparently, things were going quite well for him. They lived in a beautiful brick home complete with a built-in pool—way more than she had growing up. Little did Charlotte know, however, that on a couple of his business trips alone, he was into a little more excitement than she could ever have imagined.

After we had known her a few years, she called us one day to meet on a weekend. Her voice sounded so excited. Over lunch, she told us they were going to Hawaii for a convention for one full week, and she wanted us to help choose a wardrobe. Tony told her this was a very special trip, as he anticipated another promotion and wanted her to look her best. It seemed to us that he had come quite a long way in this company quite quickly, but who were we to know. So we focused on Charlotte.

Marilyn, the fashion bug of our group, was so excited about helping Charlotte with the shopping. A few days later, we all went to the Prudential Center in downtown Boston, stopping in to various stores to choose day and evening clothes—lots of dresses, pants, and even a few tight-fitting tops. Charlotte even sprung for a two-piece bathing suit—something we never thought she would buy. Marilyn blurted out that "Charlotte is going to be quite seductive" on this trip!

When we were done shopping, we went for something to eat. Sitting around enjoying our salads and burgers, we all agreed we had never seen Charlotte so excited; the grin on her face was huge the entire time. We couldn't really tell if it was the trip or the promotion (which meant more money) that pumped Charlotte up so much, but we were happy for her no matter, for her life was good.

The day of her departure, she called us to say goodbye and to tell us she would be in touch as soon as she arrived safely. She had a thing about calling us no matter where she went. We could never figure out why. Did she want us to know she arrived safely, or did she want us to be jealous? I thought "jealous," as she loved to tell us the fancy furnishings and things they acquired too! Hey, she was a longtime friend; whatever made her happy was okay with us.

We each received a call later that day saying she had arrived safely and the weather was beautiful. She said she had never seen flowers with so many different colors and, best of all, she was greeted with a beautiful lei as she stepped off the plane. She even said she felt beautiful, something Charlotte didn't often express.

The week went by so quickly, and we were all anticipating her call to hear how everything went and if Tony received his promotion. We also wanted to hear about the food, because Charlotte always raved about the cuisine wherever she went. She was always willing to try new dishes. We used to make faces at her, as some of the dishes were not of our taste—things like calamari, liver, and raw sushi—before it was popular. She would laugh at us and say, "You guys are just not worldly."

However, more than a week had gone by, and none of us heard from Charlotte. Usually, she would be off the plane and home for five minutes when she would pick up the phone, calling each of us one at a time. While waiting to hear from her, we called each other every day, wondering what the hell happened.

"Something must be wrong," Marilyn said one evening at work, and we all agreed. Finally, she dove right in and called Charlotte.

When Marilyn called me with the report, I could've been knocked over with a feather. "Sit down, you will *not* believe this," she began, talking a mile a minute. "I called Charlotte and it took her forever to answer, and when she did, she could hardly speak, she was so upset. She said I should come over, but I made her tell me over the phone."

Charlotte revealed to Marilyn that what was supposed to be a special trip certainly was special—but not in the way she had anticipated.

It seems that on those trips Tony took alone, he became involved in a game called "toss in your hotel keys." Charlotte had no idea about this until after dinner one night when they all went down to the lounge. They were all sitting around the table when one of the men asked, "Should we get started?"

"Sure," responded one of the wives. All of a sudden, everyone started throwing their room keys in a basket on the table in front of them.

"Tony tossed ours in," Charlotte told Marilyn, "and as naive as it seems, I had no idea what was going on, even when someone announced, 'Do not pick up your own; if you do by mistake, toss it back.' I looked at Tony, and he appeared to be very excited. I said to myself, 'Well, maybe he will explain.'"

Charlotte started crying a bit on the phone to Marilyn, and when she composed herself, she continued. "Boy, how naïve I was. But I guess no explanation was necessary, as the next thing I knew, Tony got up from his chair with a key and left me sitting there. One of the wives said, 'Honey, has he not told you what we do with these keys?' I said, 'No, of all the trips I've been on, we've never done this.'" Again, Charlotte started to cry a bit, and Marilyn just waited until her friend could go on.

When Charlotte continued, Marilyn couldn't believe it either. "That nice wife explained it was called 'wife swapping' for the evening," Charlotte explained. "She described it as 'innocent fun,' saying if I didn't want to participate for the first time, it was okay. She told me there is always someone else who passes 'for the first time.'"

Marilyn went on with the story. She said Charlotte began to cry again. "My husband has been doing *this* on his trips? Why would he make me look like a fool and take me along full well knowing I wouldn't participate in anything like this? I was left sitting there by myself, not knowing what to do next. So I went back to my room praying no one was there. Thank God no one was, but I had no idea where my husband was."

Apparently, several hours went by at the hotel that night, and Tony finally came in.

"I shouted, 'What the hell is going on, and how could you even participate in something like this and bring me along?' He said, 'This is the corporate world and evidently you don't get it.' I could not believe this man I loved would even think of asking me to do this or that he would do it himself. Could I have not seen this?"

At that point, Charlotte's voice turned cool. "Marilyn, I really have to think things over, that's why I haven't been in touch with you and The Girls. I don't know what to do."

"You don't know what to do, Charl?" Marilyn immediately said. "You get rid of him, that's what you do! What if he gives you a disease or something? Are you crazy?" That was Marilyn, right to the point.

I didn't even have a chance to comment as Marilyn told me this story, not that I know what I would have said. But Marilyn continued. "I couldn't believe she has to think about what to do. He probably has a past that we know nothing about. Remember this was a quick trip to the altar."

I finally dug deep and forced some words out of my mouth, though it was hardly much considering how intense this story was—and how far from my view of reality and relationships any of it was. I simply said, "Marilyn, we had better call her in a couple of days to make sure she's okay." Then I hung up my phone and, to this day, I think I am still shaking my head.

Charlotte did not leave Tony after the incident, and while we couldn't imagine her staying with him, we just assumed she felt she had nowhere else to go; she lived a nice lifestyle and didn't want to give that up, especially after growing up with little. We assumed, however, that she paid a huge price for staying. After that episode, she seemed a little distant, and then never mentioned it again—nor did we.

It was quite a while later, but one day Charlotte called and asked us to meet her for coffee. She had something important to tell us and wanted our opinion. Marilyn couldn't wait, as she loved gossip, but Bella and I felt sad that Charlotte had stayed with her husband, so we were not quite sure we wanted to hear her news.

"How bad can it be?" Marilyn reassured us. "Maybe she has decided to get a divorce after all and is going to rake him over the coals."

Charlotte selected a small coffee shop downtown from where she lived. We had all met there a couple of times for coffee on Sunday mornings. It was quiet and never crowded. When we three arrived, Charlotte was already seated in a booth. Her face was serious and she looked extremely nervous. We all sat down.

"I needed my friends to tell me I have made the right decision." She wrung her hands on the table. "I have decided to leave Tony."

We sat there for a moment with our mouths open, as we never really imagined her making this decision. Charlotte began to cry, folding her face into her hands. Bella passed her a tissue. I stood to hug her. Marilyn blurted out, "Congratulations!"

When she could compose herself, Charlotte told us the story. She had been talking with an attorney and had been checking around for places to live, which she never dreamed she would ever need to do. "With the help of friends, I think it's going to be okay," she said, quietly. "But it will be so different."

"I think you should fight to keep the house," Marilyn said. "After all, you are entitled—you have the children and--"

"No," Charlotte cut in, shaking her head. "I really want to start over with a new life and new adventures, nothing from the past."

We all sat silently a moment. This was the most Charlotte had ever shared with us in all the time we knew her. We were always the ones who were telling her about our past and adventures. After all this time, it was nice that she opened up and felt more emotional and human like the rest of us.

I broke the silence: "Group hug!" They all looked at me for a minute, and for the first time in many encounters, Charlotte actually opened up her arms! We all laughed and cried a little and, as usual, Marilyn said, "This calls for a celebration." We knew then, Charlotte was going to be okay.

CHAPTER 3

BELLA'S BIG FAMILY FEASTS

It was a beautiful sunny afternoon. The sky was bright blue, a gentle breeze was coming through my screen porch door and I was just getting ready to sit down and enjoy my cup of coffee when the telephone rang. It was Bella. I could hear the clanking in the background and I knew she was cooking one of her dozens of Italian specialties. I could practically smell her basil-infused marinara sauce over the phone. I was a little surprised she was calling, because she was always so busy all the time with her children, her husband, and her Mom, who had come over from Italy to live with Bella after her Dad died. Bella had her hands full all the time, but you would never know it. Her personality was always bubbly.

"Hi my friend," she began. "What are you doing—how about coming over to the crazy house for a good time and a good meal?"

My mouth watered as if I could taste the food. "Are you going to make your special rice balls?" I asked.

"Absolutely, if you're coming," she said. "Sorry for the short notice. I intended to call you last night but the kids and I got caught up in a video and before I knew it we were all asleep."

"You don't have to ask twice," I quickly said. "I'll be there." They lived in a small two-bedroom home in East Boston but it had the largest kitchen ever, which is why Antonio bought the house. Bella didn't care about the size of the rooms as long as she had a good-sized kitchen and a huge backyard. She believed a happy cook in her kitchen made a happy home. She was also of the mindset that as long as the weather was good and not too cold, everyone ate outside in the fresh air. I guess that came from her Italian roots.

I finished my cup of coffee, although I knew a cappuccino would be waiting for me when I arrived (she made the best). On my way there, I stopped to pick up a small bouquet of flowers for Bella, because even though she had every flower and bush imaginable in her backyard, she loved to receive flowers. I remember her telling me that once in a while, on his way home, Antonio would pick up a small bouquet, and even though she would say "What are you buying flowers for?" she was so happy with his thoughtfulness. I wanted her to know how much I thought of her.

When I arrived, I could almost smell the sauce from the driveway. Bella came running out with her cooking apron flying in the breeze and her children running alongside. We all hugged and kissed on both sides of the cheek (as was her usual greeting). She said Antonio was in the backyard with his brothers setting up the tables and chairs. We walked toward the house and I could hear lots of Italian conversation. It was Antonio's brothers, Angelo and Giuseppe (I always loved their names), a few friends, and Bella's Mom, Isabella. Isabella had only been here for a few years and knew very little English but was always trying to teach everyone Italian.

Oh my God, as I got closer to the house, the aromas coming from the kitchen made me so hungry. She had her sauce boiling on the stove, her freshly made pasta on the cutting boards ready to be tossed in the water, large bowls filled with green salads, chicken cutlets frying in the skillets turning golden brown, and plenty of Italian bread lying on the counters. She had to keep guard on the bread as Antonio, without fail, would grab an end of the bread and dip it into her sauce.

Immediately, Antonio rushed in. "So glad you came," he said, giving me a hug and a kiss on each cheek, European style. "This is the only time Bella makes her rice balls," he added, laughing his usual good-hearted laugh. "She always tells me they're too much work to make just for me."

He invited me outside. "Everyone's here, although I'm sure you heard the noise coming up the driveway!"

As I went into the backyard, everything looked so nice. The long tables, the chairs, and her best china and silverware were all in place (no paper or plastic in this household). Everyone laughed and talked in a mixture of English and Italian. It was straight out of a scene from *The Godfather*. Antonio's two brothers and their wives and children had already arrived. Antonio brought Bella's Mom over to say hi. She told Antonio to tell me that she had heard the laughter in the kitchen and knew I had arrived. She was a very small woman with curly brown hair like Bella's, and the most beautiful olive skin. When I met her for the first time and mentioned her beautiful skin, she told Bella to tell me that it was from "the sauce, wine, and good Italian air." Antonio said, per his mother in-law's insistence, that he put her chair between mine and Bella's.

I became so caught up in the moment outside that I forgot my cappuccino, and the next thing I heard was Bella yelling from the kitchen, "Jodi, your cappuccino's ready." Antonio yelled back, "We gave her a wine." I laughed. It was like being in the North End with people yelling out of their windows. I found myself yelling back to say, "I'll be right in to help you."

The food was almost ready and everyone, including myself, went into the kitchen and carried out the many, many dishes. Everything not only smelled good, but once the food filled the table, all the magnificent colors resembled a magazine cover. As Bella made her entrance into the backyard, her face glowing with approval, Antonio yelled with hands raised, "Everyone, take your seats, it's time to *mangi*."

Isabella stood up with her glass raised and, asking us to raise ours, said, "A familiari, amici e la buona vita." (To family, friends and the good life.)

Indeed, every visit to Bella's was so fulfilling, as

I was surrounded by family, friends and the good life. Of all The Girls, I think Bella filled an extra special place in my heart, perhaps because she was so much younger than me, and, having no children of my own, I valued time with other people's families. Whatever it was, Bella's inclusion of me that day, and other days, warmed my heart.

CHAPTER 4

THE GLORY DAYS WITH MARCEL

While Charlotte, Marilyn and Bella were married, I was the only one who was unattached—or so they thought. A few months into our friendship, I revealed the story of my long love affair with Marcel.

I met him soon after starting work at a part-time job that was every young person's dream at that time: working in a candy company. I worked until eight every evening, and the people in the office were a lot older and treated me really well. I answered the phone and helped with typing and copying. We didn't need to get dressed up for that night shift, but I always went in my Evan Piccone suits and other best clothes, hoping they'd offer me a full-time job. The only downside to the job was getting home at night, because I needed to take two different buses, sometimes waiting a long time for each, and it seemed to take forever to get home.

One extra-interesting piece of the job was the handsome day-shift supervisor. He was in charge of fixing the candy machines upstairs and keeping them running. Back then, I was tall and slender, with dark brown hair that I wore long and pulled back in a ponytail and I liked that he seemed to notice me. I remember one evening when he came down to ask me to do some typing for new charts. I thought to myself, "What a nice-looking man!" He had a nice nature about him and spoke with a wonderful accent—he was of Armenian descent and had a hint of French in his speech. I was so excited Marcel had asked me, personally, to do something for him; you would think he was the owner of the company!

However, I had heard a lot of stories about him. He had been married, had children, and was a womanizer. The women in the office could not say enough bad things about him.

Not long after he asked me to do the typing for him, it was raining very hard one night after work, and I was getting soaked at the bus stop. A Blue Eldorado drove up, rolled down the window and a man asked, "Can I give you a ride?" It was dark, so at first I couldn't see who it was. The man yelled out the window, "Hey, it's Marcel from upstairs, can I give you a ride?"

"No thanks, my bus is coming soon," I quickly replied. Thank heaven at that moment the bus arrived, as I honestly don't know what else I would have said if he asked again.

The next day, I went over to my co-worker Beverly's desk and gushed. "You will never believe who stopped at the bus stop and asked me if I wanted a ride—Marcel from upstairs, he..."

She cut me off in mid-sentence. "Stop, no more!" she began. "Haven't you heard all the things we've said about him? Also, he's much older than you and do not be fooled by the charming accent." I knew she and the others were just trying to protect me from a man twelve years older, but I kept my little crush under wraps anyway.

Several weeks went by and he neither came down to our office nor did I see him anywhere in the building. I figured he was insulted because I hadn't accepted his ride. I was disappointed but didn't say anything more to my co-workers.

About three months later, it was pouring pelting rain, and he came by in the car again, rolled down the window and said, "Well, Jodi, do you think you want to take a ride, or is your bus coming?"

I didn't hesitate. "You know, I think I'll take a ride. The bus is overdue."

"Just give me the directions to where you live," he said. I climbed into the car and somehow I wasn't nervous this time. The candy company was in Somerville and I lived in Cambridge. We had about twenty minutes together.

As I settled into the car, I said, "I hope I didn't hurt your feelings last time."

He paused, then replied, "I understand. I'm sure you've heard a lot of stories about me during my divorce. Now you can tell me why you *did* get in the car this time?"

"You were one of the nicest people to me at the job, and I didn't want to hurt your feelings again, so I thought I'd get in the car." I looked down at my hands while talking at first; I was having a difficult time looking right at him, because his face was so handsome it made me shy. Finally, I looked right at him and said, "I think it's kind of sad when people divorce. It's awful because I know you have three young children."

He talked slowly and carefully, his voice warm. "It's just something that happens."

I listened quietly and then told him he couldn't drop me off at my house. I still lived at home and I knew my mother would be upset because of our age difference. He had to leave me at the corner of the street at the bus stop. He hesitated, but agreed.

I remember walking down the street saying to myself, "Oh my God, he's so nice."

I left that job about one year later and went to work for a bank in Boston, working the evening shift, 6 to 11 pm, where I met "The Girls." One time during the coffee break, after they'd been asking why I never married and didn't have children, I finally said, smiling, "Because I have a boyfriend." They nearly died when they heard how much older he was.

After that first ride, Marcel drove me home a couple of times and one time he asked if I would ever go out on a date with him.

"We don't have to tell anyone," he said. "I'll just take you out to dinner."

I agreed, and I told my mother I was going out with my friends. But he had asked me to get dressed up because we were going to The Ship in Lynn, and I can remember my mother saying I was a bit dressy for going out with my friends. I just shrugged and said, "We felt like dressing up, Mom."

I even arranged for one of my friends to pick me up at the end of the date and drive me home.

That night at The Ship I was a nervous wreck because it seemed so far from home. When we arrived, it struck me as a real "grown up" place, from the reservations, the older crowd, the reserved dining area, and even a dance floor. I can remember him asking me to dance and, despite my hesitation, I recall the song "Lady in Red" playing, and as silly as it sounds, I still think of that night whenever I hear that song. I thought I must be in heaven.

We were only out there for few seconds when I felt uneasy.

"Marcel, I better sit down," I said. I was so nervous I thought I'd faint! He led me back to our table and we sat down. I explained that this was all new to me, and he was understanding. I stirred my Pepsi—I hadn't wanted a drink, because the date was so exciting to me I didn't want to spoil it by drinking.

Meanwhile, my girlfriends were so excited about this—it was the greatest thing to pick me up and take me home. In their car, later that night, I swear I swooned.

Years later, when I told this story to The Girls, they were thrilled! They thought it was so incredible that I snuck out to be with Marcel all those years. And when they eventually met him, Marilyn was enamored with him of course—she liked all men, particularly someone as handsome as Marcel. Charlotte thought he was hot, because he's got that foreign look and accent—Charlotte loved accents. But my good old friend Bella, well, she was apprehensive because of his age, even though he'd never shown his age, and our age difference was never an issue, until more recently.

I continued to date Marcel while still living with, and later taking care of, my mom for nearly ten more years. And although she figured things out about me and Marcel, we never talked about him because we both knew she didn't approve.

Not long after she passed away, when I was in my mid-thirties, one day Marcel said, "Jodi, let's get married."

I told him that I treasured the relationship, but that I preferred moving into my own apartment for the first time in my life, without anyone else to take care of, and, besides, I liked my independence. I reassured him that we would continue to see each other several evenings a week and on most weekends. He understood. I think, in the back of my mind, I also didn't want to go against what I knew would upset my mother.

Marcel and I often went to the beach on summer weekends, and he talked periodically about making a trip back to France, where he had grown up, having come to this country in his late teens to live with an aunt in the United States, to experience a better life.

"How would you feel about traveling out of the country with me?" he asked one day.

"I've never been out of the country," I replied, sitting up on my beach blanket and listening curiously. "I don't even have a passport."

"That's not a problem. We can get that." He said he'd love to take me back to where he lived because he hadn't made a trip since he came to the United

States and would love to show me his old neighborhood and where he came from.

I listened with a big grin on my face; I thought it was a grand idea. Marcel soon sent me for French lessons to learn to communicate in France, and we went into Boston for my passport.

Two months later, in early July, we were buckled into our first class seats on Air France, flying from Boston to Paris. He wanted to show off a bit for this trip, thus the first class tickets. I remember being so excited I couldn't even find my buckle in the seat! And when asked if I'd like a drink, I turned it down because I wanted to be sure I could take everything in with all my faculties. On this first trip—yes, this was the first of many return visits— we rented a car in Paris and drove all the way to the south of France, stopping in Montpelier overnight, then driving the rest of the way to a town called Cassis. Marcel knew of a hotel there, The Bostuan, near his hometown and right on the Mediterranean. When we checked in, they thought we were married and on our honeymoon, so they gave us a room overlooking the water. I thought I'd died and gone to heaven. Marcel and I always enjoyed lovely dinners, and we found a favorite French restaurant, sitting at the same table year after year, looking out at the water and the bustle of people walking by. I still remember sharing the delicious bouillabaisse and drinking a Cassis red wine made right there.

A few days into our trip, we took a drive to the neighborhood where he grew up. He was as excited about this first trip as I was so he could show me all these things from home. Although no family remained, many friends still lived in the neighborhood. We saw his family's apartment, still there, and the bar he used to go to; we even encountered a taxi driver he remembered.

He enjoyed that month-long trip as much as I did. It was a wonderful, wonderful thing he could share with me, and I was enamored with him each and every day.

From then on, I never saw "The Girls" during the month of July, because Marcel and I went back year after year and stayed in the same room in the same hotel for one month every summer for nine years. The hotel owners became like family. I still remember the little things they did for us, like making me a boiled egg for breakfast every morning—after I taught them how. And every day, one of the waiters of the restaurant they owned right across the street by the beach would place a mat out for me to use later in the day—when the beach was crowded and mats would have been difficult to find.

All year long, we couldn't wait for the month of July; even though we did lots of fun things at home, it was nothing like July when we could be together in a romantic environment morning, noon and night.

On one trip, while visiting a grand church on a hill with a spectacular view, I said to Marcel, "This is a wonderful place for someone to get married."

"Do you want to go ahead and finally do it, Jodi?"

I laughed and said, "Not today." I think he's still shaking his head in bewilderment because it was clear I would always skirt this issue.

It turned out that was our last trip back. Our fun

and romantic relationship continued and our lives settled into a comfortable routine, even moving in together a few years ago, but I still miss our trips. Recently, despite Marcel's advancing age which has slowed him down some, we began to discuss one more trip. Who knows, maybe we will try again one more time.

Marcel and The Girls only met a few times, but I'm glad they all knew each other way back when, and it's nice to revisit some of the most special years of my life.

CHAPTER 5

WINDING DOWN AT THE BEACH HOUSE

The Girls and I kept up our fabulous friendship for nearly twenty delightful years, with our ties strong, since we all still worked for the bank and saw each other all the time.

Sadly, the moment we all dreaded eventually occurred. By then we were in our fifties—Bella of course much younger. For some time, there had been rumors that the bank was to be bought out by a larger bank, but we were hoping that, even if it were true, they would still keep a night shift, which we four worked all those wonderful years.

However, when the new bank took over, they eliminated the night shift. We could have applied for full-time day jobs, but most of us already had day jobs, or families that made the night shift ideal. It was late June and we had until the first of September to take the severance package offered or apply for a day job. We knew that we were all going to take the package, as a job at the new bank was not an option for any of us.

Charlotte, Marilyn, Bella and I decided to do something special—not that we ever needed an excuse to do something special—because we didn't know where this change would take us all. We hoped to keep in touch of course, but we suspected it wouldn't be as easy. So Charlotte, who had remained single after her divorce and in her quiet way liked to cook up fun ideas now and then, suggested a night to do it up special—with a sleep-over.

We all laughed, and Marilyn, Bella and I each said, "We're not kids anymore!"

"You don't have to be a kid," Charlotte said. I remember her standing near our desks looking so sure this would work out. "We can have a lot of fun and laughs," she said, working us over. "When was the last time any of us did something like this?"

Bella spoke up first. "I don't know if this will work for me because I have such young children and, besides, I've never stayed anywhere without my family."

Marilyn joined in. "This will just be another night out with The Girls, Bella; we just won't go home after. We're not kidnapping you forever!" We all laughed.

Bella said she would discuss it with her family, and we all thought it was a good idea. But where would we go?

Charlotte popped up with an idea. "I have a friend with a place on the beach. I'm sure I can convince her, given the circumstances. I'll bet she can let us borrow the house for a night. What do you think?"

We all liked the idea and told Charlotte to ask for it and let us know. We decided a Friday night was best, as that was the night we usually went out sometimes after work. We also thought August would be grand as the weather should be good.

A week or so went by and we were all eager to learn if this plan would work out. We only had another few weeks together on the job. Finally, Charlotte told us her friend said "yes" and we could go the first Friday in August, not long after I returned from France with Marcel. The only rules were that we needed to bring our own food, leave the place clean, and not have any wild parties.

"No wild parties? What a bummer," Marilyn said laughing.

Bella thought her husband would agree to this. I was beaming, so excited with this plan. Marilyn asked if the house was big and had plenty of bathrooms. Charlotte rolled her eyes and said, "Just wait until we get there—you will see for yourselves!"

The day finally arrived, and it seemed we were going away for a weekend instead of an overnight! Bella drove so we could all fit in her van. Marilyn, true to her personality, packed tons of clothes, makeup and accessories—way more than she would need. We were like a bunch of kids going on holiday. We were so lucky: it was a beautiful day, sunny and warm. We blasted the music and all sang along. I remember thinking to myself, "What a great bunch of girls," and I hoped that we would all keep in touch after that final day of work.

After riding for over an hour and a half, we

started thinking we were lost, when all of a sudden Charlotte screamed, "Turn on the next road!" We nearly passed it: the road was not paved, and dust flew everywhere. "What a long driveway," I thought, and I hoped Charlotte really knew where we were going.

In the distance, we saw what looked like a massive house, and as we got closer, we parked and all climbed out, the smell of the ocean immediately assaulting our senses. What a great feeling!

"It looks grand," Marilyn announced, and we all agreed.

The house was a big old Cape Cod style home, and we approached a beautiful long stairway to the front door. Marilyn practically barked, "Someone has to help with my bags!"

We all laughed and then Charlotte announced, "No valet service here!"

"We're probably not going out; why did you bring so much?" Bella asked.

"Well we have to eat!" Marilyn quickly replied, assuming they were going out.

"We sure will eat!" Bella announced. As a surprise, she had brought all the food for a wonderful Italian supper.

"Wow, Bella, we must have been on the same page," I said. "I brought the wine!"

Charlotte piped in: "So did I!"

We knew then it was going to be a great time, and indeed it was.

Not long after, the bank let us go. I worked as a secretary, then a pharmacy technician, and finally settled in as a legal assistant, which seemed to be my niche. Bella decided to stay home with her children, husband and favorite place, her kitchen. Charlotte went to work in a library full time, which suited her as she was an avid book reader and liked quiet surroundings. Marilyn was in a new romance—her two husbands had both died young, so she sold her home and bought a condo, inviting a much younger man to move in with her. She decided to stay home and enjoy herself.

We kept up our get-togethers every couple of months for the first years, but with time, this began to change. Our schedules all differed so much, and even though we called each other once in a while, we became busy with our own lives.

We hadn't seen each other for nearly a year when we finally managed to get together again. It seemed to be eternity. It was amazing how different we all were at this meeting. It was almost like we had nothing to talk about. Maybe, in the past, working together for so long and talking about ourselves and the people around us had given us things to discuss.

We all seemed older at that visit, held once again in the North End, but simpler, not at our usual restaurant, just somewhere convenient for all, which I even forget. I do remember, however, that we were not those carefree young women we once were. The conversation was forced and Charlotte and Marilyn seemed a bit more removed.

Little did we know that this would be the last time we got together. Marilyn, Bella and I called once in a while, but we never heard from Charlotte again.

Eventually the friendships faded away. The loss of these companions has been huge for me, and I realize this more and more as I age and look around for people to have that level of fun with again. Being young and carefree is a unique time in life, and I miss it with all my heart and soul, but that is the nature of our lifespan, perhaps.

CHAPTER 6

AN UNEXPECTED PHONE CALL

One summer day a few years ago, the phone rang as I was getting ready for work and buttoning my blouse in the apartment I shared with Marcel. I grabbed it. It was Bella. We had not all been together, or even in touch at all, for probably fifteen years. Circumstances had changed for a couple of us, and we seemed to go our separate ways.

I had a feeling this call was bad news just by the sound of her voice. Although we were both briefly happy to reconnect after the lapsed time, she quickly said she was calling with sad news.

"Oh Jodi, Marilyn has passed away," she said. A terrible feeling came over me, and I fell silent for a moment. I told Bella I had to sit down.

She had no details about Marilyn's death, but luckily she had seen the notice in the newspaper. It seems funny that years ago we used to tease Bella, the youngest of the group of course, for reading the obituaries daily, but how fortunate that she had kept up this practice.

Bella said she had a difficult time tracking down Charlotte due to her name change (of which we had not been aware), but finally found her, she thought. She said she had left a message, along with her telephone number, to get in touch, but hadn't received a response yet.

The wake was that night, with the burial the next day. Bella suggested we go together to the wake and she would pick me up. I gave her my new address and directions, and she said she would pick me up at 7:30 pm.

As I hung up the telephone, my head was swirling as to what could have possibly happened to Marilyn. She would have been nearly seventy. Marilyn had been so full of life, and took such good care of herself. She absolutely loved life. The last I had heard, some ten or fifteen years earlier, she had married the younger man she had been living with—assuming that, as she got older, he could take care of her. She had purchased a condo with him, although I am sure she, alone, had paid for it. We had all met him prior to the marriage at one of our regular monthly get-togethers, but we were not impressed. Marilyn always wanted to show off her "conquests," but we felt this one she could have done without! We knew—although Marilyn would never notice—that he felt he was doing her a favor, coming to meet us that day. During that lunch, we noticed a few things that he said about Marilyn which he deemed funny, like comparing her white slacks and navy blue blazer to a sailor. "I'm going out with a sailor," he boomed one time. How insulting! But she laughed, which made us feel worse because she allowed him to get away with insulting her. Needless to say, we didn't find these remarks humorous at all. Bella and I actually announced that we didn't think it was funny, and Marilyn brushed it off, saying, "He's only fooling." We never said any more about him; we just figured that if she was happy, that was all that mattered.

However, we were not invited to that third wedding of Marilyn's, and we didn't hear much from her after that—only an occasional phone call, and then nothing.

The day of Bella's sad phone call, I went to work, but my mind was elsewhere. I thought how sad it was, after being so close, that we never knew there may have been a problem with Marilyn's health.

When I walked in from work, my telephone was ringing. It was Bella saying that Charlotte still had not returned the call and she would pick me up at 7:30 pm as scheduled. I heated up a cup of tea and thought to myself that I wished I didn't have to go. I have a thing about wakes. People always look so different from what you remember, and I was hoping Marilyn would not look anything but beautiful.

I started to get ready, and it was so ironic—as I tried this and that on, Marilyn's voice in my mind seemed to say, as she had so many times as I tried things on, "You must wear that!"

Soon, the doorbell rang, and there stood Bella, my old friend. She was still her bubbly, happy self, just a little bigger than I remembered, although she and I were always more focused on loving ourselves just the way we are, than working at keeping fit like Marilyn and Charlotte had been. We hugged immediately and I realized how much I had missed that; we were the two huggers of the group.

"Wow, Jodi, you look the same." Bella said.

"So do you."

"Just a little bigger from my Italian cooking!" We both laughed. I asked how Antonio and the two children were.

"I now have three," she said, with a smirk. I was totally shocked, because she had once said she'd stop at two. Hmm...the frisky Bella had not changed. We talked nonstop from the apartment to the car to the funeral parlor. Then almost like magic, we both stopped talking at the same time, avoiding going inside. I guess we were both feeling the same way. Bella finally whispered, "We have to pay our respects to our old friend."

We walked up to the front door and you would have thought we were walking to our death, we were going so slowly. The young man opened the door for us and showed us where to go. Bella whispered, "Boy, Marilyn would have liked to have checked him out." I smiled. It was true; Marilyn was always eyeing the fellas no matter where she was. Bella and I looked around but didn't recognize anyone. Unfortunately, Charlotte was not there.

As I went to the casket to say a prayer, I looked at this friend of so many years and said to myself, "What happened old friend?" She certainly did not look like the fashion plate of old.

Bella, as usual, was talking to a few people; she could join in conversation at the drop of a hat, and I knew she wanted to find out what happened. A friend that lived next door to Marilyn said that husband number three had left a little over a year ago and had taken quite a bit of money out of Marilyn's accounts. She had noticed Marilyn going downhill after that—drinking more and not taking care of herself. The woman said she heard Marilyn had a heart attack. Bella and I both knew from years ago that Marilyn never wanted to be alone. She always needed a partner. We knew then, in spite of it all, she had died of a broken heart.

We left happy that we had gone to the wake, but sad at what we saw and heard. Bella said she was going to try and keep in touch with me, and if she heard anything from Charlotte she would let me know. Boy how I missed those girls, I now realized. Marilyn, in her vibrant years, was always exciting, and Charlotte, despite her reserved manner, was a warm and trusted friend.

As I closed my eyes that night, I recalled that dancing was Marilyn's favorite thing in life. I said out loud, as though talking right to her, "Marilyn, I hope you are happy now and you are dancing in heaven with the angels."

CHAPTER 7

MEETING AGAIN IN HEAVEN

Since Marilyn's funeral, Bella and I have not been back in touch, and we never located Charlotte—or she might have chosen not to get in touch with us, who knows. I'm not sure why Bella and I let things slide; maybe I waited for her to call, and she waited for me to call. Or maybe life just got in the way, who knows. Much as I miss those glory days, I guess Bella and I decided to let it all just settle in our memories forever. I even tried to reach her recently, but she no longer lives in the same home and had no forwarding information. At that point, I remembered what the four of us used to say: that someday, we would all meet up and have some more crazy times in Heaven.

So I imagined what this will be like for us someday...

"Oh my God," I said out loud as I arrived at Heaven's Gate. It was more beautiful than I could ever have imagined. Walking on those fluffy clouds was so peaceful and calm I almost thought for a minute I was dreaming! Until, in a distance, I spotted beautiful tall gates glistening in the sun...and my wonderful friend Marilyn standing at the gates with a glass of Merlot in hand. She looked as good as I remembered her years before, her hair styled fashionably and makeup around her bright blue eyes.

As I approached, her face lit up. "How do I look?" she asked, then answered her own question. "Pretty good, huh? My heavenly gown is beautiful but a little big, don't you think?" We both laughed, and then she took my hand as she said, "Come on in. You'll be amazed at who is here, and the people are all so nice."

As she led me around, we approached a table with a red checked tablecloth and a small unlit candle. The table reminded me of the old days in the North End of Boston, and I practically expected to see Anthony, the owner of Dolce Vita, but last I knew he was still doing well on earth. The table came into better view soon, and there were my other two friends, Charlotte and Bella, sitting at the table. They stood and we all hugged, except for Charlotte, who laughed and backed away—still not a hugger! "She hasn't changed one bit!" Marilyn said.

We all began to laugh hard as we sat down at the table, and then all the emotion turned to crying tears of joy, although I was also sad to learn what had happened to all of my friends: Marilyn had, indeed, died of a broken heart; Charlotte had moved in with one of her children, living out her years there; and, sadly, Bella died young in a car accident.

Always the good hostess, Bella poured the wine and we all toasted to "Friends Forever." We clicked our glasses so hard we thought they might shatter, until we remembered it was heaven, and only good things occur. Just then, as we were talking and laughing, a handsome man—a total stranger who was tall, dark, and brown-eyed—appeared out of nowhere and headed right over to Marilyn. Apparently, her magnetic sex appeal persisted in Heaven.

"How about introducing me to your friends?" he asked. We all glanced at each other with smirks on our faces. We were all thinking the exact same thing: how good it was to be together again, with so many new adventures ahead....

*Everyone should have a
"Remember When" in their lives.*

-- by Judith Adele Yarbrough

ABOUT THE AUTHOR

Judith Yarbrough is a retired Registered Pharmacy Technician now working in an IP Law Firm. She is the mother of two beautiful cats, Molly and Maggie. Since childhood, Judith has written lots of short stories and has always wanted to be published.